It's Halloween Night!

For my mom, Lee Barrett,
whose creativity has always been an inspiration
—J.O.

To Beverly and Charlie
—J.M.

Text copyright © 2012 by Jennifer O'Connell
Illustrations copyright © 2012 by Jennifer Morris

Library of Congress Cataloging-in-Publication Data is available

ISBN 978-0-545-40283-5

10 9 8 7 6 5 4 3 2 1   12 13 14 15 16

Printed in the U.S.A. 40
First printing, July 2012

It's Halloween Night!

Written by Jennifer O'Connell
Illustrated by Jennifer Morris

Cartwheel
·B·O·O·K·S·®

SCHOLASTIC INC.

New York   Toronto   London   Auckland   Sydney   Mexico City   New Delhi   Hong Kong

It's Halloween night and I'll be a fright!
With this pointy hat and my spooky cat,
I'm a …

It's Halloween night. I'll dress in all white.
I've cut out two eyes for a big surprise.
I'm a ...

GHOST!

It's Halloween night. Won't I be a sight?
With a coal-black nose and fur head to toes,
I'm a ...

It's Halloween night. Watch out, I might bite!
With these scary fangs and my pointy bangs,
I'm a ...

It's Halloween night. My costume's just right.
With my satin gown and golden crown,
I'm a ...

It's Halloween night and the moon shines bright.

We run through the gate and can hardly wait.

On Halloween night!